dragon legacy: the apprentice

Mave Hathaway

books by mave

Dragon Legacy

The Apprentice

Training Camp (Publishing August 2025)

Baelian Empire

Dodsfell Chapter

The Breaking

Death of the Wolf (Publishing September 2025)

United We Fall (Publishing 2026)

...more coming soon...

For the kids who dream of riding dragons.

praise for the apprentice

"I read this with my youngest son and asked him for his thoughts and this is what he had to say.

'I really liked this book and want to read more about Ozzy and his dragon. The book was easy to read and I liked that Ozzy is a normal boy like me who likes to go on adventures and help his mum. The book reminds me of my favourite movie 'How To Train Your Dragon' because they found each other and became best friends too. I would give this book 5 stars.'" - Bo-Maree Stuart

"This is such a lovely story about lifelong friends and the curveball that life has a tendency to throw. Highly recommend for kids of all ages." - Em Fyre

"I fell in love with little Ozzy straight away! A curious boy who can't avoid adventure even when he tries. When he stumbles upon a friend in the woods, he unknowingly opens a world of excitement, fear, magic and wisdom. Most importantly, he finds a friendship to last a lifetime, maybe more than one!

This is a perfect novel to read to your little ones or to start your new chapter book reader off!" - AL

prologue
Five years Ago

Delia tiptoed into the birthing chamber, awe filling her at the sight of her best friend with a miniature embodiment tucked into her arm. Her friend's head came up with a jerk, alert and wary until she realized who was entering the room.

"Come closer it's alright I won't bite."

A satisfied warmth spread through Delia as she neared the new pair. It had been a rocky few years of their friendship. They had agreed that settling down in the secluded village was the right option but as time flew by, at a rate much faster than Delia had anticipated their friendship had begun to fizzle out. Other responsibilities had taken priority over their relationship. It would be one of her greatest regrets, but the news of the next generation had gone a long way in healing the fracture.

"She's beautiful. You're going to be the best Mum. The council chose well." Delia leaned in examining the newborn.

"You act like they had a choice."

Humor and joy filled the room, palpable to even the baby who gurgled and cooed in her Mum's arms.

As she watched the new family Delia was transported back to when she had met her friend and their bond had solidified. It had been a moment of such intense emotion that using words to describe it seemed inadequate. Delia's life prior had been lived on the edge, in a world that was unable to handle her reckless urge for adventure. Yet, when her friend had met her gaze for the first time the world had shifted under her feet and it became obvious that her life changed forever. The idea that she would never be alone again no matter what happened was reassuring for someone who had navigated the initial years of adulthood feeling lost and alone.

Delia reached over to caress her friend's face, pride and love filling her mind. "You should know I'll be there for you, no matter the situation. Thank you for trusting me with your little one."

Her friend's eyes glistened with tears, "We won't be seeing each other very much I'm afraid. This little girl will take my time away from our friendship."

Sadness filtered in as Delia finally understood what was happening. She bowed her head, resignation and under-standing pouring into the air around them. She choked back her own tears as she nodded. "You know that's okay. This little one deserves the world and you will make sure she gets it. If you need me you know where I am." Delia tapped her chest lightly right over her own heart. Her friend nodded and turned her attention to the baby who had begun to cry, perhaps picking up the emotions floating in the room.

Delia leaned over and kissed her friend on the forehead and stroked the baby's cheek, a silent goodbye. As she left the birthing chamber she turned back one last time taking in the sight of her lifelong best friend, a feeling filled her that their story wasn't finished. Time would tell.

one
Missing

S he stomped through their cave, hunting. Immott's nose was flooded with the smell of babies. In any other instance it would be perfectly normal and wanted, yet right now it distracted. Shendri her wayward independent daughter, had disappeared. At least Immott was fairly certain she was gone. The fact that her smell pervaded everything made it much harder to find the tiny sneaky girl.

She roared, her fear spiked as she nuzzled the various leaf piles that Shendri loved playing with and hiding in. Her favorite pastime was to burrow into the leaves and wait until she sensed Immott nearing and then popping out and causing a spike to Immott's heart rate.

Her mind raced as she replayed the afternoon. Everything had been normal. As the sun had begun its descent Immott had left after giving Shendri explicit instructions to stay put. The cave was where they would be safe from the evils of the outside world. After all Shendri was only five years old and for their species it was still much too young to communicate effectively. It left her with only one assumption, someone must have taken her.

Immott left the cave lumbering out to the forest. Her mind wrestling with many different thoughts. *Why would someone want her baby? What was happening to her? Was she scared?* Immott was so focused on her thoughts she didn't even feel the trees brushing her body. One thing Immott knew for certain was that she could and would find her again.

All she had to do was get to the road. Then she could make the humans give her back. They would be desperate to do what she wanted once they realized they were stuck in that tiny village of theirs.

two
Birthdays

Ozzi sat up eagerly. His mind shouted loudly about all the joy that this day would bring. Today he turned ten years old, a magical age that he had been waiting for because it was when adults finally started taking children more seriously.

Ozzi slept in a bedroll next to his parents bed, his twin sisters taking up cribs on the other side of their bed. Most mornings everyone took extreme care to be quiet so as not to disturb anyone else who happened to be asleep. Yet today, he bounded from his bedroll uncaring for his noise aiming straight for the table. The excitement over what his parents left out on the table for him. Usually they left a present or two along with a delicious sweet treat. The treat only ever happened on birthdays due to their cost and he couldn't wait to experience the explosion of flavor on his tongue.

He crashed into the table unable to stop his forward motion due to the excitement filling his entire being. The echoing thump of his hands knocking the chair into the table echoed through the quiet room, undoubtedly reaching the bedchamber where his family all slept. He took a deep breath closing his eyes hoping no one but especially his sisters woke up due to the noise.

Once it seemed that no one had heard him, he focused on the table top. Disappointment zinged through him. There were no presents and no delicious sweet treats. His mind flooded with worry. *Had they forgotten his birthday? Were the girls more important?* He shook his head refocusing. Instead of worrying he looked around the room. The fire was still banked, and the curtains which normally beckoned the sun into the room were closed. Curiosity getting the best of him Ozzi peeked out and realized that the day had barely begun, the sun not yet fully visible.

Soft footsteps padded behind him, causing him to turn. His mum stood hand on hip, a shawl pinned around her shoulders. "Ozzi my boy, you are up far too early."

"But mum it's my birthday!"

She chuckled softly. "I had no idea that was today. The countdown you've been keeping the past week didn't give it away. Turn away and close your eyes my boy. You aren't old enough to learn of my hidey holes for gifts."

Ozzi laughed, clenching his eyes closed so tight it hurt. He could hear a cupboard open, the hinges creaking, wrapping crinkled as his mum had to be placing the gifts on the table. After a few minutes his mum cleared her throat. "Alright my boy you can open your eyes." Ozzi did his heart jumping at the three lumpy packages and the chocolate cake.

His mum grinned. "You know this is probably the last birthday where you won't have to share your treat. The girls will be old enough next year to eat some. If they wake up early, I guess you'll have to either share or be more quiet when you wake up." She threw a wink at him.

Ozzi grimaced a bit before he nodded "Yes mum."

He finished the chocolate treat, diving into the packages. There was a long package that was rather lumpy, a medium rather fat package and a small really round one. Ozzi had guesses for the two out of the three packages opting to open the one that had his curiosity peaking the most, first. He gripped the long lumpy package and ripped the paper off of it. A large coil of leather flopped out landing on his lap with a flop. He couldn't stop the frown from gathering on his face. *Why would he get a coil of leather?*

"It's a belt! You've been growing so much lately I got one big enough to fit you for a while." His mum clapped her hands excitedly.

Ozzi quickly morphed his frown into a smile, doing his best to seem grateful. He reached for the next package. The medium one if he had to guess was going to be some sort of clothing. He did his best to mentally prepare himself to smile. He ripped the paper open and shock radiated through him. He stared open mouthed at a small basket with a spade and small paring knife. Everything was shiny and new a very different sight. Usually his gifts were second hand and while it didn't matter it added another layer of awe to the gift. "MUM!"

She grinned, her eyes leaking a bit. "I know how much you love foraging so we saved for better supplies."

"It's perfect!" Ozzi knew exactly how he wanted to spend the day.

His mum pushed the last gift to him and he smiled. He knew this gift, it was honestly hard to not know what it was. It had to be a ball. He ripped open the paper and a satisfied smile filled him as the ball rolled onto the table top. He didn't really understand why his mum had gotten him one though. He wasn't a very active sports child, he much preferred to explore and learn than throw a ball around. He cocked his head confused. He gave his mum a small smile. "Thank you."

"It's so you can play with the girls more often. They love rolling things back and forth, this way you can all enjoy."

Understanding filled him. He was grateful to have something to do with his sisters, it was so hard to know how to play with them when they were so small. "That makes sense Mum. Thank you for my amazing birthday." His Mum squeezed him in a hug and kissed the top of his head.

"Be safe today Son. I shall see you back for dinner, your lunch is packed up on the counter." She moved back to the bedchamber heading to start her day fully.

Ozzi grinned. A whole day to explore the forest. He couldn't imagine a better way to celebrate.

three
Mushroom Hunting

Leaves crunched under his feet as he walked through the forest, full of curiosity at what could be waiting around the corner. Ever since his Mum gave birth to the twins, Ozzan Madigan had become more and more familiar with the woods behind their cottage. His excuse to his Mum and Pa revolved around the collection of edible mushrooms and berries to aid in contributing to the house while the babies were young and needing more hands-on-care. Since the twins had come along, he had seen tons of wondrous creatures, foxes, deer, and once he observed a family of rabbits. His favorite part of the day was coming back to the cottage and describing all the things he had seen to his baby sisters.

Occasionally, he stumbled upon things that led more to punishments than praises. Much like the one time he plucked a bundle of plants to gift to his friends. Being the kind lad he was, he thought they would be an edible treat for all. Instead, all of their parents complained when their children had broken out in rashes that itched abominably. Ozzi's own Mum had to go and barter with Mistress Delia, the village's elderly healer, to get an itch balm for everyone involved. It had cost them a month's ration of sugar as they had to direct the funds typically used to purchase the sugar toward the cost.

Similar small instances consistently followed Ozzi around and, despite his good intentions, he always ended up in trouble. He was determined to put all that behind him now, as today was his tenth birthday and he was well on his way to becoming a man. He expected that soon his Pa would take him along on jobs, teaching him how to earn for the family.

He wandered aimlessly in the forest, casually kicking at the leaf piles built up around the bases of tall trees. This forest was on the very edge of the village and, as the last cottage on the lane, he had always felt comfortable wandering throughout. After the misfortune with his friends, his Mum had taken the time to teach him which mushrooms were good and safe. She had also shown him other edible plants that could aid in supplementing their diet. He loved being surrounded by the trees and underbrush, the natural noises of the forest were quite calming. A rustling in a nearby pile of leaves made Ozzi stop and wait. Perhaps he could catch the family a rabbit for dinner. His Mum would surely celebrate such a meal.

The rustling grew louder and he heard, no felt, a sense of curiosity that wasn't his own. He scrunched his face, confusion filling him because his own thoughts weren't making sense. While frozen in indecision and confusion, a silver, scaly head popped out from the pile and snapped him immediately out of his stupor. He stumbled backwards, tripping on a branch and landing in a heap on his bottom as his mind translated what he saw in front of him.

"What...?" he whispered, intent on not startling it as he leaned closer, having never in his life seen the color silver glistening on a creature of the forest. Even the snakes he occasionally caught were more brown or green in coloring, aiding in their ability to camouflage. Nothing in nature was silver except... his brain stuttered upon the word for a moment and then he breathed it out on an exhale giving a name to the wondrous creature in front of him, "Dragons."

The dragon in front of him was quite small, if in fact it was a dragon. Its head was about the size of his own baby sister's head but more triangular in shape. Its ears were large, floppy, and almost translucent, similar to the wings which were now visible. The leaves fell away as the creature wiggled in excitement over the inspection. Ozzi's brain blanked as he realized he could feel her excitement. His own enthusiasm at this discovery began to grow, mirroring hers.

"Well, hello!" he spoke loudly, his own elation getting the best of him.

She jumped vertically a solid foot, aided by a flap of her wings, as she startled at the sound his voice made.

"Oh! I'm sorry, I didn't mean to scare you." He modulated his tone to be softer and less obtrusive, closer to what he would use to talk to the babies. Confusion filled him, he was fairly certain someone had told him that dragons could talk. "Don't you talk? Use words like me?"

The small creature in front of him tilted her head and then he saw a vision of a large dragon inside his own mind. This dragon in his thoughts was familiar, it was a much closer image of Immott, the village's protector. Yes, he was *seeing* a vision coming from the small one before him.

"You can't talk now, but will when you're bigger?" he asked, hoping she could understand him.

A feeling of joy and success filled her, causing Ozzi to smile widely. Somehow he had found a dragon and was successfully communicating with her. A more special birthday moment would be impossible.

Realization struck as his basket hit his side, he couldn't stay out here with her forever. Soon he would need to return home and be with his family. A jolt of sadness flitted through him as he considered explaining her to Mum and Pa. Dragons, while not unheard of, were incredibly rare and would bring attention neither of his parents would want. He only knew of the one dragon, the one who had taken over protection of their village. Shaking his head at the thought, he opted to shove it to the back of his brain and turned to his new friend.

"Well little one, would you like to come with me as I hunt mushrooms?" He pointed to the ground at a mushroom. "I need to find a good armful, if possible, to bring to Mum to make up for being out with you all day. I bet you could smell them if you wanted to help." He got down on his knees and brought his face up close to the mushroom and inhaled deeply. "See, smelling. Then you smell the air." He demonstrated, despite the fact that he himself wasn't able to smell a mushroom from dank leaves. Then, pretending to use his nose to lead him, he found the next mushroom and picked. "Make sense?"

She glanced up at him but Ozzi hid the mushroom he was holding behind his back, curious to see if it would work. She stumbled around turning in a circle and then dove her head straight into a pile of leaves at the base of a tree. She pulled her head up and sneezed once more, levitating a few inches before settling back down. He approached slowly, certain she had found a mushroom.

"May I look?" Ozzi leaned down and she started as his nearness, backing up quickly. He spoke softly, not looking directly at her, "It's okay, little one. I don't really know what else to call you but I feel like you're a girl. Little One is a good girl nickname. I should know; I have sisters, you see." He began to smooth the leaves out of the way of the mushroom which was, in fact, nestled there. "Oh, see! You did great! Thank you so much, Little One!"

A thought fluttered through his brain quickly, so quickly he couldn't be sure if he made it up or if it came from her. *Shendri.*

He plucked the mushroom, adding it to his threadbare pack and said, "Shendri. Is that your name?" He could see her from the corner of his eye and she didn't seem upset. In fact, he felt a wave of joy come off of her. "Well, I'll call you Shendri until you can tell me if I'm wrong." He nodded and began to dig under the next tree looking for another mushroom.

Ozzi heard Shendri turn and wander away and he was filled with a sudden sadness. The idea that he wouldn't see her caused distress to shoot through his brain at an alarming rate. The feeling of sadness quickly resolved at the sound of her sneeze. He brought his head up and saw her a few trees away pawing, as he was, to uncover more mushrooms, these bigger than the last. "Oh! Thanks, Shendri. My mum will love these so much."

The afternoon melted away with more mushroom hunting and various explanations to Shendri on what all the different plants were. The sun slipped to half mast and his pack was heavy before he remembered he must return home.

four
Hiding

"Oh no." Ozzan stopped suddenly and looked at Shendri who was getting more comfortable with him. She still kept a bit of distance, but she followed faithfully behind him. He also felt her emotions with alarming accuracy.

Shendri cocked her head and chirped.

"I have to go home soon. How will I leave you alone? How will you stay safe? Not everyone in the village is as nice as me, you know. Dragons are so rare that one sight of you at your size, you'd be passed around like a doll."

Shendri grunted and startled back.

"No worries! I wouldn't do that to you! Yet, there are those that would. I will find someplace safe for you." Ozzi looked around at where they had ended up in the forest. They were near a cave that was up a small hill and very well hidden from anyone wandering around. How was he going to get her to stay in the cave? He peered into his pack, already knowing that there wasn't anything inside of it that would be helpful. However, he spied a likely aide as he looked down to where his belt secured his pants to his waist.

The belt was a length of leather knotted around his waist.

It wasn't fancy but it happened to be pretty long. His Mum hoped he would be able to wear it for a long time. It had been his birthday present only this morning. Ozzi grimaced slightly, imagining his Mum's reaction to him returning home without it, but it would have to do. The process of unknotting took a bit of time. His Mum had triple knotted the thing, making it almost impossible to remove. Shendri tilted her head and watched avidly at the new activity, unsure of what Ozzi was up to.

"Well Shendri, I'm trying my best to get this knot undone. You see, if we want to make a safe place where you can't wander into trouble, I need to tie you up here."

Shendri let out a loud high pitched squeal of protest, backing up slightly.

Ozzi groaned. "It's okay, Shendri! I promise. I won't hurt you. I'll come back and make sure you have food and keep you company. It'll be okay. It's just to keep you away from the villagers." He pulled the belt off and his pants sagged a bit in response. "You see that hill?" He pointed to the hill that had a small rock fall on the face of it. "You'll be safe up there in the cave. It's pretty big, too. So you won't be cramped." He took a few steps forward, holding the leather strap. "I promise I won't hurt you, Shendri."

Ozzi felt regretful about tying Shendri up but he wasn't sure what else to do. His Mum would banish little Shendri to the cold like she had with the kitten he had brought home once before. She did not tolerate animals in the home, especially since the babies were born. Shendri rippled with emotions of confusion, sadness, and fright that she expressed with crooning. She began to back away rather slowly, with two big but gentle steps, Ozzi was much closer to her. He moved fast, desperation cresting through him as the sun lowered further.

Ozzi leaped, landing on his stomach as his arms clung

around Shendri's neck. He pulled her closer to him and she reacted instantly, rearing back and pulling against him. Shendri used her wings to protect herself, battering him as she tried to free herself. He closed his eyes in an attempt to maintain the connection with Shendri.

"It's okay, Shendri. I am doing this to protect you. It's going to be okay," he murmured to her as he doubled down on getting better control of the situation. He managed to pull himself up onto his knees as he struggled to get the leather strap fastened. In the struggle, Shendri managed to get a few very well placed swipes of her talons, a shallow graze on his arm and a much deeper one on his leg. Once the strap was fastened, he sat back breathlessly holding only the end of the strap.

"I'm sorry, Shendri! I really am, but did you have to hurt me?! I'm trying to take care of you. If I had a choice I wouldn't choose this." He gingerly touched a scratch running down one arm. He sighed heavily and looked up the hill toward the cave. "Can you just walk up there with me, please? I promise it'll be okay. I'll come visit after I sleep. And you can rest, too. I promise I'll even bring you some food! I'll prove to you that this is best and you'll be safe."

He stood slowly and took a few steps in the general direction of the cave. The strap went tight as Shendri scooted backward from him and the cave, crooning again. Fear filled Ozzi's mind. The fear was so potent that he began to cry softly. "I promise, Shendri. You'll be out of harm's way in the cave."

He tugged once more.

She shook her head.

Ozzan sighed and pulled. It was hard work and, at times, he had to brace his feet to pull with both arms.

The sun was well into the trees by the time they both made it up the hill, spitting mad. Ozzi wiped at his forehead, a streak of dirty sweat coming off onto his arm. His leg stung from the sweat as did his arm. Shendri, once a translucent silver, was now brown and dull looking. A thick layer of dirt kicked up when Ozzi tugged her up the hill. Shendri was making a sound so shrill, so loud and sharp it hurt Ozzi's ears. He continued to drag her toward the cave entrance while pleading words of comfort and trust so he could fasten the leather strap to a rock within.

"Come on, Shendri. We are almost in your new home. Then I will go get us some food and return, I promise."

Surprisingly, she accepted and went with him, needing very little convincing to continue on into the cave.

In an overwhelming show of gratitude, Ozzi exclaimed, "Oh thank you so much, Shendri. Thanks for coming in here so nicely." He fastened the lead to a rock formation near the front of the cave which allowed her to wander in and out as she saw fit.

As he turned away, a feeling of satisfaction filling him, Shendri pounced. She went straight for his thigh and gripped it with her mouth chomping down, using her paws to claw at his legs. Ozzan yelled, tears of pain bursting out as he fell down. At that moment, a new sound entered the scuffle that truly made Ozzi's blood run cold.

"OZZAN MADIGAN!!"

It was a very familiar female voice. When she used his full name it was a clear indication that she wasn't in the mood to play.

He used as much care as he could to pry Shendri off of him before rolling out of reach. As he headed toward the mouth of the cave, he felt a sudden and unexpected heat hit his back. He yelped and danced forward, away from the flames. Whirling around, he saw smoke curling from Shendri's mouth and felt satisfaction emanating from her. His tunic was a bit crispy in the back as he danced around trying to see the damage.

"Shendri! Mum's gonna kill me! She can't fix this or pay for new ones! Oh no. What will we do?" he huffed, tears leaking out once more. "I'll come back tonight and we will make a plan. We have to find a way to work this out. And I promise I'll bring food."

"OZZZIIII!!!" The call echoed around the woods as he made out the faint cry of one of the twins. Dread filled him; she had come to find him and dragged the babies with her.

"So much for returning home to praise," he muttered as he looked at his full pack and back down at his ripped clothes. Sighing and downtrodden, he straightened his shoulders as he limped down the hill. The dread of his Mum mixed with the pain that Shendri had caused him welling inside.

five
Consequences

Ozzan kept his head low as he walked down the hill. He followed the sound of his Mum's voice and found her with one of the babies tied to her back and the other nestled into the crook of her arm. He cleared his voice and toed at the leaves as his Mum took a sharp inhale.

"Ozzan Madigan! What happened to you!?" She rushed to him as fast as she could with two babies around her. "Who did this? *What* did this?" She plucked at his torn tunic and breeches. "This will take a lot of time to mend, laddie. You know better, Son." There was a long pause which caused him to finally look up into her face. He quickly looked away as he realized she had grown quiet to restrain her anger. Her voice cold and somewhat distant, she asked, "Where is your belt, lad?"

He swallowed hard and did what he hated most; he lied. "You see, Mum, I was out getting all these mushrooms." He brought out his pack which was teeming with fungi. "During the process of crawling around I musta lost it. It musta loosened and slid off. I swear, I didn't notice until shortly before you called out for me. I tried to find it. It's why I'm late, you see." He glanced up to see if his words were having any effect at all on her countenance.

Her mouth, however, remained a firm line and the furrow on her brow, which only came out when he or his Pa had done something to vex her, was still there. She reached out and cuffed him upside the head. "You are a terrible liar, Ozzan Madigan. Get ye back to the house, ye rascal. We'll see what your Pa has to say to that."

Ozzi swallowed another mouthful of lies knowing the damage was done if his Pa was going to find out. He hung his head in gloom and turned toward the house, limping a few steps forward before he looked back. He saw his Mum staring, open mouthed, tears gathering in her eyes.

"Ozzan, what's happened to you?" Her voice broke with emotion.

He furrowed his own brow, uncertainty filling him. "Whatcha mean, Mum? I told you I was off picking mushrooms..."

"And a tree set you on fire, did it?" she demanded, interrupting his tale. She rushed up behind him and with a delicate touch, traced the burned patch. "Get in the house now. I shall see how bad this is and determine what we should do. Don't think I missed that limp, boy. I saw it and I'll be seeing that leg when we get in near the fire, the sun's too far gone now for me to make it out."

He audibly gulped. This was not the ending to his birthday he had foreseen, that's for certain. Through gritted teeth, he made his way into the house as quickly as he could to minimize his limping, and relieve the pain radiating up his leg with each step he took. Shendri had definitely ensured he wouldn't forget her presence in the cave.

Once they all entered the cramped cottage, his Mum freed herself of his sisters, depositing them in their bed. It had always resembled a cage to Ozzi but it did a great job of keeping his rolling sisters confined and away from the danger of the fireplace. Much like Shendri, they needed to be kept out of danger by confinement. He moved to start on his normal chores, which included gathering more firewood for the night and setting their places at the table, but his Mum interrupted him, "Not so fast lad, turn your back towards the fire. I want to see this back of yours."

He moved slowly, reluctant to hear how bad it truly was let alone have to lie once more about how it came about.

She groaned, "Ozzzzaannnn. How did this happen, Son? Is someone harassing you? Are you okay? Did you do this yourself?"

He didn't know what to say exactly so he remained quiet.

"Let me see your leg now, Son."

Wordlessly, he pulled up his breeches and turned it so the injured area was facing the fire. Down his pale leg was an open oozing cut, it looked rather deep but the cut was also very dirty.

"No. No, this won't do. I have to take you to see Mistress Delia. We have no options." She huffed out a breath as she glanced around the room noting their obvious lack of funds. "Hopefully I can barter our way to your medicines. I don't want to risk you getting any worse. Let me step into the neighbor's house and then I'll take you to Delia's."

She took off her threadbare apron and patted her hair.

Ozzi groaned, "No Mum, it's fine. Totally fine. Don't bother the neighbors, I'll be fine. I promise. It's just a bit of scratches, all will be well in the morning." He turned to gather the wood for the fire and grimaced a bit as the turn stretched the skin awkwardly.

"Nope, that's it. Stay here and watch your sisters, I'll be right back." She was gone before he could protest again. He huffed out his breath and looked at his sisters who were cooing and whacking each other with their little club-like hands.

His Mum came whirling into the room moments later; their small elderly neighbor came in behind her. "Thank you, mistress. I shall bring you some dinner tonight as payment. I shan't be more than an hour and then I'll be back. Their Pa will be home soon."

Ozzan backed away towards his sisters. "No Mum, no it's fine. We don't have to go."

"You'll listen to me, young man, and get yourself over here right quick." When he didn't move, she advanced on him with intent clear on her face.

He flinched away from her, expecting a cuff across the back of his head. Instead, she struck quick as a snake, grabbing his ear lobe and twisting. He yelped, "Owwww!!!"

His Mum, however, showed no sympathy as she began to drag him out to the main lane and on towards Mistress Delia's shop.

six
The Healing

Delia looked out into the town square and noted that the lantern lighters were making their way down the lane. She would keep her doors open no more than another hour and then she would make her way to her soft bed. Her old bones couldn't continue standing the entire day, tending to the various ills and injuries that their small village saw. She needed to get herself a likely apprentice, but sadly hadn't seen any evidence of anyone up to the

She looked up from pounding herbs to see an odd sight. Little Ozzan Madigan was being dragged across the town square by his mother who had, what appeared to be, quite a grip on the lad's ear. She smirked at the sight, knowing that Ozzi was a boy well-known for getting into trouble, some of his own making and often the making of others. She looked away from the sight, reminiscing a touch on her own childhood full of innocent misunderstandings, when the sound of the bell on her shop door tinkling caused her to look up once more.

The smile on her face grew just a touch at the sight of

Ozzi, half bent to the left, with his mother gripping his ear, identical scowls on both their faces.

"Mum, leave off. It's fine, there's no reason to come here."

"Ozzan, you will tell me where these cuts and burns came from at once, young man! I can't believe I have to force you to get them tended. The one on your leg is still bleeding, for heaven's sake, Son! Just think what the neighbors will say. They will think we cut you or burn you for discipline." She paused in her tirade before adding in a mutter, "Don't think I haven't considered it, just to get you to listen, of course."

Delia cleared her throat, casually tucking some fallen white hair behind her ear while swallowing a chuckle, before stepping fully into the parlor of the shop. She inclined her head in respect to Mistress Madigan and Ozzi before stepping closer to them. "Well, hello there and welcome to my shop. How may I be of assistance?" She directed her question to Mistress Madigan as Ozzi was frantically shaking his head. Well, he attempted to but as he turned too far away from his mother's grip, he halted in a growl of pain.

Mistress Madigan released her recalcitrant son and sent him a glare that would freeze someone twice his size before curtsying to Delia. "Good Evening, Mistress Delia. I am hoping to barter a trade."

Delia nodded. It was a common enough practice in their small community, bartering for services when coin was low and for tenant farmers such as the Madigans, it was usually low. "Well what type of services will you be needing this evening?"

Ozzi's mother shot him a glare that could injure before gesturing helplessly at her son. "He won't tell me," she sighed and shook her head slightly. "That's not entirely accurate. He is bleeding from multiple places as far as I can tell. It has eased into a sort of oozing now but that can't be good. I've also seen a burn on his back but he is now refusing to show me."

Delia's eyebrows rose at the list of injuries. She turned to Ozzi and asked, "What have you been into, lad?"

Ozzi remained stubbornly quiet, staring at the ground. She began to walk closer and noticed that a faint ooze was leaking out of his trouser leg on the right and onto her nice hardwood floors. He looked rather worse for wear. The Madigans were never rich but they kept their children well dressed in clothes without rips or tears, yet all of his clothes had small holes. Eerily like talon holes from an owl or a... her eyes went wide as she realized what it must be.

Delia reached out her gnarled hand and pried up his chin, making the child look her in the eye. "Ozzan Madigan. You will tell me what you have done."

His mother noted the change of tone and her anger at her son flared once more. "Ozzan, if you don't come clean this instant I will tell your Pa and good luck to you." She crossed her arms in front of her and tapped her foot impatiently.

Stubbornness flared within Ozzi's eyes and Delia, in all her years of wisdom, knew it was time to change tactics. She walked to a cupboard and pulled out clean clothes. As Mistress Madigan started to protest, Delia just shook her head with a smile. "Now, Mistress. Young Ozzan here needs a bit of time to understand the situation, to process, you understand. Why don't you head on home," she spoke softly as she looked out to see the sun falling fast. "Your other wee ones will be needing their supper after all. He can stay the night and I shall see him safely home once we get to the bottom of this."

His mother looked between him and Delia. "I can't pay for him to stay that long." She swallowed hard and looked to the ground. "What will you be wanting in exchange, Miss?"

Delia looked Ozzan up and down and made a rash decision. "I've been needing an apprentice to help around the shop. You know I am advancing in age, dear. Perhaps Young

Ozzan can be of assistance, if we can get to the bottom of this little issue."

Ozzi jerked at her words, being brought back to the present moment, his attention having strayed to thoughts of Shendri. Surprise colored his words as he exclaimed, "Seriously, Mistress D? You want me?"

She smiled and nodded slyly. "Depends on what sort of trouble you have found yourself in, mister."

Ozzi looked sheepishly at the floor.

His mother cuffed him upside the back of the head and took a grip of his ear once more.

He whimpered and bent to her will.

"You will behave for Mistress Delia, young man, or you will pay for your insolence when you get home."

As she released him, he nodded violently. "Yes, Mum. I promise I will make you proud."

She gave him one more glare before dropping into another curtsy, making her way out of the shop.

Delia handed him the new clothes and gestured to the back of the shop where a spare room was situated. "You shall change and gently rinse the wounds. I want you then to roll up the right pant leg." She pointed to the oozing appendage before adding, "I shall need to see the cut to know what salves will work best."

He nodded and shuffled into the next room. It took but a few moments to change into the new clothes. He sat on the bed and revealed his leg wound, grimacing at the sight. It hurt, but he was excited at all the new possibilities. Worry rolled around his head as he considered if he should tell Delia about Shendri. He had heard that she was a trustworthy person but other than a few times when he needed healing, he hadn't spent much time with her. He squared his shoulders as he stood, preparing to walk out and show her his leg. He would keep an open mind and perhaps share his news of Shendri, if the time was right.

seven
Learning

Ozzan couldn't relax into his new duties as an apprentice to Mistress Delia. His mind bouncing between concern over Shendri and fear of Mistress Delia's expected interrogation over his injuries. All she did though was dress his leg wound and apply a salve to his back, not once requesting any further information. Once it was dressed and cared for, she had her maid, Marie, bring him some supper and then she shooed him off to bed.

The next morning, he was sent on a bunch of errands around the village delivering packets of various herbs and potions. This stunned him. She didn't ask him one thing! His Mum would have interrogated him until he broke down due to annoyance, yet Mistress Delia simply went about her morning as usual and expected him to do the same. He was also stunned with the freedom that came with being her apprentice. He was allowed to go anywhere that her customers had need and no one thought twice about it once he explained his new position. The possibilities he could have if he managed to stay on with her were endless.

As he wandered through town, he barely spared a

moment's notice on the men folk gathering in the middle of the town square. His attention was finally caught when yelling broke out from the center of the group.

"Gather your weapons!"

"We have to fight!"

Ozzi stopped short on the edge of the gathering and watched them warily. His brain raced. *What fight? What is happening? Is the village safe? Should I alert my family?*

They lived in a quiet little village that was protected by a dragon. While the dragon itself was scary, their community was always reliably protected. Nothing ever bothered them. He noticed his former school teacher not far down the lane from him and wandered over. "Mr. Wynn, Mr. Wynn, what's happening?"

Mr. Wynn grumbled under his breath, "Just run along Ozzan. It's a bunch of troublemakers, that's all."

"But Mr. Wynn, please, what's happening? Are we safe? Is the village in danger?"

Mr. Wynn grumbled more, shaking his head. "Oh, Ozzan. It's the dragon, Immott. She's turned against us for some reason. Her bonded mage can't get through to her and the headstrong people of the village are leaning into some terrible ideas."

All the blood drained out of Ozzi's face. "Immott is attacking the village?" he asked, his voice shaking.

Mr. Wynn shrugged sadly. "At this point, lad, she is only attacking those who dare to leave. These hot-headed men think she will begin attacking us. I've lived a lot longer than most of them and I am sure a solution will be found. Just focus on yourself for now, laddie, and let the adults figure it out."

Ozzi nodded slightly before inclining his head respectfully to run back to Mistress Delia's shop.

He entered yelling, his words coming out in short loud

bursts, "Mistress! Mistress D!! Have you heard?" As he came around the door he noticed that she was standing at the window, pounding some herbs while the patron sat talking to her on the couch. He paused in his yelling, suddenly shy and afraid to speak of what was happening in front of this newcomer.

Mistress Delia looked over at Ozzan and raised an eyebrow before turning back to her herbs. "Ozzan, love, go check in with Marie and get some lunch, my lad. Once you've eaten and I'm finished with Mistress Charlotte's order, we shall talk."

Ozzi opened his mouth to argue but a side eye from Mistress Delia, as if challenging him to do just that, halted him in his tracks. Instead, he chose to follow her directions and headed toward the kitchen, his head hung low.

It took about thirty minutes before Mistress Delia finally entered the kitchen, taking her mortar to the sink. "Alright, Ozzan. Now that we are alone, what is it you wanted to tell me?"

Ozzi looked around and noticed that Marie had left somewhere. Delia lowered herself to a seat, groaning a bit as she settled onto the wooden chair. Ozzan startled. "Are you alright, Mistress?"

"Oh yes, Ozzan, just my old bones creaking with age. No need to worry about me. You, however, came tearing in here like you had caught fire. What is it that ruffled you so?"

"I saw the men all crying for battle in the town square. They are going to go after Immott. She's been attacking those trying to leave."

He watched as Mistress Delia got more contemplative at this news. "That is a bit concerning, lad. Yet, we can do nothing about it. We don't know what she wants, and we have very little sway with the men." She shook her head sadly. "We shall just have to increase our stock of burn balm. A perfect first recipe for a new apprentice." She went on about how to make a salve and the differences between salves and lotions but Ozzan had begun to tune her out.

His mind wandered to Shendri and his concern over her safety deepened. If the men of the village felt brave enough to go after Immott, a fully grown dragon, a baby wouldn't stop them. If only he could talk to Immott. He straightened up a bit and asked, "Who is Immott's bonded mage? How does one become a bonded mage?"

Delia trailed off her rambling of burn ointments and gave him a curious look. "A bonded mage is a human that is chosen by the dragon in question. Then, after they get to know one another, eventually they are able to mind-speak with one another. The mage also gains a wider range of power, as well."

Ozzi hung on every word, excitement filling him at this explanation. "Yet, who is the bonded mage linked to Immott? Shouldn't they be able to calm her down or find the solution to make her happy?"

Delia chuckled a bit at his eagerness. "My, my, so many questions. I forgot just how eager the young can be. One key thing to know is dragons live an awfully long time and will frequently out-live their bonded partners. Once their bonded partner reaches a certain age, they withdraw contact to make the passing of that partner more bearable, you understand. As it is, Immott's current partner is too old to hold a steady connection. Immott will not take another partner until her current one passes into the great beyond so she's rather unreachable."

Ozzan became contemplative himself, the joy and excitement fading as the reality set in. "Mistress Delia?" He paused a bit before asking, "Didn't you say that her bonded partner can be connected to her occasionally, just not as frequently?"

Delia paused before answering, "Well, yes, that's true."

He sat up straight once more. "So it is important to know

who it is! That way we can get some sort of information about her!"

"Perhaps. We shall have to see but until then let's see about this salve." Delia stood slowly and began to gather various implements around the kitchen, explaining as she went. Ozzi tried his best to internalize what she was saying, still hoping she would finalize her offer of apprenticeship. He also mulled over how he could best help the people of his village, while still protecting his new friend Shendri.

eight

Feeding a Dragon

Ozzi worked the rest of the day making and preparing the ingredients in a daze, thinking over all he had learned and trying to find a window of opportunity to sneak away. Mistress Delia, however, had other plans and kept Ozzi incredibly busy through the day. He was so exhausted around the time Marie was plating up supper that he struggled to keep his eyes open during the meal. He smiled half heartedly at Marie as he toyed with the roasted chicken and turnips on his plate. As slyly as possible, when the women at the table were busily eating their own food, he pushed bits of chicken into his lap and onto the waiting napkin. He felt pretty confident in his deception when Mistress Delia noticed his rapidly emptying plate. "My, my, so hungry tonight. Marie, he's such a small lad, is there enough for him to have some more?"

Marie gave him a warm smile. "Aye milady, I suppose we could give him another helping. It won't hurt the pigs to miss a meal now and again in support of a young lad's growth." She heaped more onto his plate and his eyes widened at the bounty. The initial helping had been more food offered to him in one sitting than his entire life. And now, he was seeing more! An abundance of delicious, hot food. Ozzi devoured this helping, fully forgetting his attempt to put food aside for Shendri.

Once he had finished his second helping, Mistress Delia insisted that he head off to bed in his new room. Marie smiled indulgently and exclaimed, "We shall let you settle in before chores are decided on but don't expect to always just eat and then sleep, young man."

He smiled and nodded along to Marie before heading to his new room to settle into sleep while Marie and Mistress Delia tottered around, cleaning up.

Once he was out of earshot, Marie turned to Delia. "The poor lad thinks he needs to hide food away to make sure he eats enough! Perhaps we should send over some to Mistress Madigan. I had no idea they were in that much trouble."

Delia picked up the dirty dishes from the table, walking them over to Marie at the sink and taking her time to think out her response. She had her suspicions on the squirreled away food but she wasn't ready to share them. "Perhaps we should give him some time to adjust before we ask. I would hate to embarrass Mistress Madigan if this is simply a result of Ozzan not trusting us. I shall gently inquire when I go over to her house to finalize his apprenticeship."

Marie nodded thoughtfully. "Yes, that makes sense. I do hope she accepts help if she needs it."

Delia nodded along, murmuring her agreement.

After what he was sure was hours, he gathered his napkin of food as quietly as possible, as well as the flickering candle off the nightstand. Juggling the napkin, candle, and his shoes, he eased the front door open and slipped through the gap, turning and closing it painfully slowly behind himself. He slipped his shoes on before he made his way down the lane and cut across the town square. He was filled with a sense of urgency as he navigated the dark with nothing but his flickering candle and food for Shendri, heading for his parents' cottage on the edge of town. From there it would be simple to find his way back to Shendri in the cave. It took a few minutes to see the familiar crooked fence in the distance. Once he arrived, he skirted the fence and entered his familiar woods.

It was almost instantaneous; the feelings of ravenous hunger mixed with anger that rippled through him as he cleared the fence line and grew closer to Shendri. Ozzan doubled over at the assault on his feelings from this outside source, struggling to control his own body's response. He even found difficulty in lifting the napkin to let the smell of roasted chicken drizzled in gravy pervade the area. As he did so, he whispered, "Shendri... I'm sorry I am so late, but I brought food. I did, I brought you food. I promised to take care of you, see?" He took a few staggering steps forward as the feelings invading his brain changed slightly, ravenous hunger now mixed with curiosity.

He managed, through halting steps and many platitudes, to get to the cave entrance where he threw the napkin of food down on the ground. Moments later, his shiny new friend stepped into the moonlight, standing aggressively with her teeth bared. At first sight of the food Shendri had already begun to smell, she released her caution and pounced with eagerness and a voracious nature he hadn't been expecting. Her sounds of noisy chewing filled the air and then it was gone and replaced with a pealing cry.

"What is it, Shendri? What's wrong?" He walked closer hoping to comfort her and scratch her head.

Shendri paced back and forth while she cried. Ozzi got about a foot away from her when she leapt and raked her sharp, needle-like talons down his body. He cried out in distress. Looking down, he saw that her talons had cut through his new tunic and pants. "Why? Why did you go and do that, Shendri?!" He stomped and kicked at a nearby stump, tears flowing hot down his face. "How can I go back to Mistress Delia now? She gave me these nice clothes and gave me a chance! With her aid, I might be able to make it in the world. My Mum struggles enough to help make a way for me!" He slumped down onto his butt, bringing his knees up. He wrapped his arms around his knees and began to cry in earnest, feeling lost and unsure. After a few minutes of uncontrolled sobbing, he felt a gentle nudging on his elbow followed by a crooning. He peeked over his arm and was shocked to see Shendri nudging his elbow, her head cocked in curiosity, a deep purring emanating from her small body. He hiccuped and held out his hand, she nudged it with her nose.

Slowly, he wiggled his fingers and was rewarded when Shendri leaned into his touch.

"Hi," he murmured softly. Feelings of sadness rippled into his brain. "Are you sad? I got some food for you. It's better food than I've ever had. I'm sorry it's not enough. I will try to get more tomorrow. If she even lets me return to work." He sullenly hiccuped again, yawning widely and rubbing his eyes as he stretched. "I'll stay here for a bit and keep you company. I don't mean to leave you alone for so long, I just have to earn my food with Mistress Delia for you and for me. She may be the key to the future, you know? A future full of food and experiences I can't even imagine."

Ozzi yawned again, settling against the rock wall. Shendri chirped as he spoke, as if conversing back at him in her special language of chirps and trills. He smiled sleepily and she curled up next to him tucking her wings into her body.

nine
Discoveries

Ozzi woke up feeling more rested than he had been in his recent memory. His brain was a bit groggy and he didn't fully understand why one side of his body was warm and the other was cold. The bright light overhead was what seemed to have woken him up. Ozzi cracked an eyelid and squinted, trying to make out his surroundings. It took a minute but then he sat up suddenly, shock rippling through him. He was still in the cave with Shendri, not in his bed at Mistress Delia's. As her name filtered through his mind he looked down at his clothes and groaned. They were still ripped and ruined. He slumped against the wall, once more paralyzed by what Mistress Delia may do in response to his clothes. He heard a rustle from outside the cave entrance and Shendri sat up staring out towards the opening with her head cocked, an inquisitive chirp sounding. Suddenly, a feeling of hunger rippled off of her and an echoing pain occurred in Ozzan's own tummy.

A throat cleared and the following words made Ozzi fill with shame and guilt. "Ozzan Madigan, come out from there.

Bring the baby, even I can feel the hunger coming off that little one."

Shendri hopped onto Ozzi's stomach before he could stand, gripping him with her talons. He didn't move for fear of slicing more of his precious clothes, or worse, his skin. A few minutes dragged by while he prayed he had imagined the old woman's voice.

<hr>

"**O**zzan Madigan, I am not familiar with the concept of waiting, young man. Old I may be but I am still young enough to come in there and retrieve you. It's best if you come out on your own." Delia tapped her foot impatiently on the ground giving him another few minutes to contemplate his future. She really wasn't too terribly upset with the lad.

She had placed a simple tracking spell on his clothes at the table the night before, quite convinced all the food he was not so sneakily storing in his lap was going to end up in the gullet of the baby dragon she had been searching for on the sly. Which is why she hadn't blinked twice when he accepted second helpings of all the dishes. Marie had looked ready to question him during dinner but Delia had warned her off from commenting with merely a shake of her head. She still marveled at how a powerless boy had managed to bond a baby dragon, at first she even feared he had injured the beast. She was fairly certain that wasn't the case after his questions and concern for Immott the day before.

There was still no movement from the cave; she sighed heavily knowing it meant she would have to drag her old bones up the small rocky hill into the cave mouth after all. "I'm coming inside. Convince your little friend not to bite or she won't like my response." Delia wasn't truly worried as she had met Shendri at her hatching. Young dragons were considered infants much longer than humans. The baby shouldn't be too worried over her presence but a newly bonded dragon, regardless of age, was rather unpredictable. They were still too young to sort their own emotions, let alone handle those of their bonded partner. The fact that little Shendri had bonded with a child made the situation complicated and completely unheard of in her long lifetime.

Delia eased her old bones up the hill, trying to limit her huffing and puffing to appear more powerful than she felt, but couldn't stop the smirk when she rounded the corner and came face to face with a terrified Ozzan being held down by a dragon no larger than a puppy.

Shendri was now sitting on Ozzan's stomach staring curiously at Delia. Ozzan was frantically murmuring to her and patting her on the side as if nudging her to get up. Shendri was effectively ignoring him, staring down Delia.

"Hello, sweetie. You know, you should let him up. He has to answer some questions."

Shendri stood and stretched and then circled his lap before settling down, this time pretending to sleep.

"Protective for one so young. Yet, I think I can convince you."

Shendri's tail twitched but her eyes remained closed.

"You see, sweet little lizard, there's a nice roasted chicken in my bag that I thought you may enjoy." Delia marveled at Shendri's restraint. She reached into her bag of endless holding and pulled out the chicken container. She opened it and placed it on the ground, waiting. The only response Shendri gave was to dig a bit into Ozzan's stomach, hiding her nose with her wings.

Ozzan squeaked as, undoubtedly, the needle-like talons broke skin. He whispered something that Delia couldn't hear but he was rewarded by a series of chirps from the dragon sitting atop him. The wind shifted, enabling Delia to make out the conversation.

"Shendri. You are hungry, go eat. She won't hurt you. You were happy enough to eat her cooking last night. Remember that it was so yummy you ate it all in mere moments. Just think, all that juicy yummy meat is waiting for you," Ozzi reasoned to the stubborn lump of dragon attached to his abdomen.

Delia chuckled at the arguments put forth by a boy to his new friend. "Shendri, you know I won't harm your friend. Come eat before your mother hears that belly rumble."

Shendri sat up and, without looking at either of them, stretched and leapt off Ozzi's stomach, earning him another groan of pain before sauntering over to the chicken dish and digging in.

Ozzi stood awkwardly and bowed to Delia, his head hung low in shame. "I ... I... I'm sorry, Mistress. I didn't mean it."

Delia's brain took a minute to understand what he was apologizing for, and at her questioning expression, he gestured to his clothes and she understood. "Lad, it's all right. When you bond a dragon you must expect to go through some clothes from time to time. Accidents and all. Clothes are the least of our concerns. I do want to discuss with you what exactly you were thinking by trapping a dragon, and a baby at that!"

Ozzan scrunched his brow, the misunderstanding evident on his face. "Trap, Mistress? I didn't trap her."

Delia raised an eyebrow. "Young man, I can clearly see the poor excuse for a rope tied around her neck. Though, you should know that it's truly ineffective, she can easily move beyond that if she wants."

As if proving Delia's point, Shendri sneezed. The moment the sneeze left her body, she disappeared only to reappear five feet away at the bottom of the hill.

"You see lad, she has chosen to stay with you."

Shendri scampered back up to them and, after finding a good ray of sunshine, she settled in for a nap, her belly sated.

Ozzi gaped and his own tummy rumbled.

Delia shook her head, as if remembering that he too was but a child and needed nourishment before effective moves could be made. She opened her bag and dug out another container, this one holding scrambled eggs and sausage that were somehow still warm and steaming. She handed him the container and then found a tree stump that would work as a chair for her. "Eat up. Then we talk."

Ozzi looked between her and the food but didn't question her. Instead, he dug in and waited for something terrible to fall from her lips after his misbehavior.

ten

Disguises

Ozzan made quick work of the food she placed in front of him. Once he was done, he looked to Mistress Delia and noticed she had her eyes closed and appeared to be sleeping on the tree stump. He toed at the dirt with his boot, unsure what to say to get her attention or if he should interrupt. It was common knowledge she had once been a very powerful sorceress who had retired to their quaint little village to the benefit of the inhabitants. "Uhh, Miss Delia?"

"Hmm?" She stirred as she cracked open one eye. "All fed now, are you?"

He nodded, handing over the empty container. She took it from him and stuffed it down into the bag secured over one shoulder. He waited.

Delia let out a heavy sigh. "Now, lad. What was your goal here?"

"I... I ... I just wanted to keep Shendri safe. I didn't have any other plans. Honest, Miss. I was simply out looking for mushrooms for Mum and the wee ones when I felt it; I felt her." He looked down trying to place the words in his mind to aid in his description. "I felt sorrow, and then hunger and curiosity but it wasn't me feeling them." He looked over at Shendri all curled up on a rock enjoying her full belly and the sunshine and smiled. "She popped out of a pile of underbrush and scared me half to death. I wasn't even sure what she was, having only seen Immott from afar. I've never gotten to see a dragon up close, you know. Only mages and magical ones stand a chance around dragons and you know my story. I ain't... I mean, I don't have magic." Ozzi shrugged as if that explained everything.

Delia nodded in understanding but before she could speak he plunged on.

"I only tied her up to keep her safe from my Mum or Pa. They come out in the woods to hunt and I just knew she would hang around here. I didn't want them to come across her, or worse, someone from the village wandering back here and hurting her. I used my belt to tie her up but, honest, I wasn't trying to trap her or anger her." He rubbed his head, concern emanating from him.

Delia couldn't help but crack a smile. "Yes, she is a dragon. But she is a baby just like your Mum would see you if you were to wander off into the world without a guardian. How would she feel if I took you to a big city and just left you alone? To Immott, it's very similar. Shendri is lost and vulnerable, and with her being a dragon, there is greater risk that someone with ill intentions will steal her and sell her for nefarious means."

Ozzi scrunched his face thinking. "What's ne-far-ious mean?"

Delia nodded, glad he was asking questions, as it was proof he was trying to understand her point of view. "Nefarious means evil or with harmful intent."

Shock rippled across Ozzi's face. "I would never let that happen!"

"Ozzan. You are but a boy yourself. As much as you love

her, there is little you could do if those hunters from the village truly wanted to take her for themselves. We need to find a way to get Immott to hear us."

Tears had filled Ozzi's eyes as the truth to her words sunk in. "I would fight them." His chin was raised with a stubborn tilt to it.

She nodded. "I know, but at this time, my dear one, you wouldn't win." She tried to be gentle with her words but she needed him to fully understand the risk he had brought to his bonded partner.

Shendri would survive the loss of Ozzi but Ozzi would not survive her loss. Delia had seen perfectly healthy men die due to their dragon's passing and she didn't want to see that happen to a young one for nothing more than a childish mistake.

"This is what we shall do, Ozzan. There is no reason to dwell in what may happen so instead, let's forge a new and safer path for all. We must get Shendri back to Immott and work out with her how you and Shendri shall see one another in a safe manner. I am fairly certain Immott will be most surprised by your pairing." She looked between the sleeping hatchling and Ozzan who was standing with his hands on his hips, utter bewilderment plastered on his face.

"How are we going to do that? When are we going to do that? We can't just go parading through town with a hatchling!" Ozzi rubbed at his head, panic settling into his mind. He couldn't lose Shendri; something deep within him recoiled at the mere suggestion.

"Leave that to me, young man. I may be old but I do have a few tricks up my sleeve." She smiled warmly at him and rifled through her bag looking for something. She pulled out the necessary items, piling them next to her on the stump and stood slowly, her bones protesting. She threw a pinch of some herb upon Shendri's sleeping form causing the dragon to sneeze and raise her head. "Alright, a pinch of this. Now a drizzle of that," she mumbled as she poured some oil upon her hands and sketched runes into the air over Shendri.

Ozzi watched, amazed as the pearly white hatchling suddenly appeared as a white dog, fuzzy fur covering everything, the wings having disappeared completely. Shendri must have felt something during this process because she emanated the feelings of awe and excitement through their bond. She jumped to her paws and began frolicking in a circle, angling her head to see as much of herself as possible before rushing up to Ozzi, tongue hanging from her mouth.

Delia laughed a bit as she pulled the last item from the pile; a proper collar and leash any dog would be expected to have. Delia turned to Ozzi and proffered the leash to him with a smile. "This way we can safely bring her into the village to wait until I can get a meeting with the Great Immott."

Ozzan took the leash and smiled shyly. The kindness this woman was showing him warmed him immensely. "Do you mean I'm still going to be your apprentice? You'll still help?"

It was Delias turn to look shocked. "Of course, lad. I need an apprentice to learn the craft for the village's benefit as much as your own. Preparation for the day that I am no longer on this plane. One mistake, mind you this is not a mistake but more like a weird twist of fate, will not be used to remove you from my service. Now, go on and secure your beast. I have lots to do today."

Ozzan secured Shendri after a bit of coaxing, her excitement over her new features overriding her ability to listen. Once she was secured on the lead, they followed Mistress Delia back down the hill and past his old house into the village. He walked tall, pride in his bond with Shendri filtering through his apprehension of the meeting to come with Immott.

eleven
Settling In

The walk through town was uneventful. They didn't see anyone out of the ordinary. The men folk were still focused on their preparations to hunt Immott and, therefore, didn't look twice at Ozzi or at Shendri's disguise.

They all stumbled through the shop's door, making quite the racket. Marie popped her head out of the kitchen and did a double take at both the state of Ozzan's clothes and the fact that a white bundle of fur was hopping and prancing around his feet. Delia shot her a smile and a nod, confirmation that he was to keep the dog. Marie shot her a quick grimace before stepping fully into the room to address the lad.

Marie stood, hands on her hips in the doorway of the kitchen, turning her full attention to Ozzi and his friend. "Alright, lad. Where in the world have you been all night and how in the world did you get into such a state?"

Ozzan looked down, shame filling him. "I... I fell asleep in the woods after I found my new puppy."

Marie hummed, tapping her foot as if contemplating the fate of the two in front of her. "Well, this puppy better help in keeping down the mouse population. We all earn our keep in this house, you understand?"

Ozzi nodded solemnly.

"I shall draw you a bath, Master Ozzan, but you will be in charge of ensuring that the pup doesn't bring fleas and bugs inside. So after your bath is done, it will be *its* turn."

"She's a she, her name's Shendri, Miss," Ozzan interrupted and then his face flared red as she scowled.

"Alright then, Miss Shendri will get a bath after you, but you will be in charge of doing it. You are also in charge of cleaning up after her, mind. Only then will you both get food." Marie was firm in her statements and Ozzi glanced between her and Delia but nodded and headed towards his room.

"Ozzan, be sure you listen to Mistress Marie. If I hear otherwise, I shall be in charge of making sure it doesn't happen again." She turned her attention to Marie. "He doesn't need to worry about apprentice work today. I have an errand to run and then I shall spend whatever is left of the day in my room preparing for tonight. See that he gets some sleep, it was a long night for him, I am sure. Also, have them stick near the shop today. We will have quite the journey this evening."

Marie nodded, turning back to Ozzi and Shendri, issuing more directions while Delia slunk out the door. Her first task was to ensure Ozzi's Mum was willing to have him in a permanent apprenticeship. There would be more complications if she resisted. Delia made her way toward the Madigan cottage and smiled at the various villagers who crossed her path. She skirted the crooked fence and knocked lightly on the door, on the off chance that the babies were napping.

Delia waited a few minutes and then knocked again. The cottage wasn't large so it was doubtful that Mistress Madigan couldn't hear the knock. Which left the possibility that she wasn't at home. Delia walked around the cottage to the back gardens and there she was. Two babies strapped to her, hunched over while digging up turnips from the garden. Delia smiled at the picture of domesticity warming her heart.

She cleared her throat and smiled at Ozzan's Mum as she glanced up, shading her eyes with a dirt crusted hand. "Mistress Delia! Is Ozzan okay? He didn't work out." She looked down in an attempt to hide the look of distress but Delia saw it. Before Delia could respond, his Mum continued as she stood dusting off her skirts. "I suspected it wouldn't work but I did hope. Ah well, just send him on home and I'll console him as best I can. Perhaps his Pa can take him to the odd jobs he does."

Delia smiled widely and shook her head as she said, "No, no. You have mistaken my reason for coming! I brought the forms for Ozzan's apprenticeship to be formalized. I can go over them with you but they detail that he will learn the ins and outs of herbal healing, he will be a messenger around the village, and go on expeditions to get herbs with me." She paused letting this all settle on the stunned mother before her. "I also suspect he has some hidden magic that will benefit from some instruction, so I will be working on that with him. I won't work him to the bone, I pledge to give him one free day for every three work days. He will also be able to come visit you each evening after supper if you want. He shall send home half his wages and save the rest."

As she was talking, she had begun to hunt around in her large bag of holding and finally came up with a stack of parchment, which she had filled out the night before. Delia looked up at Ozzan's Mum and smiled at her in understanding as tears flowed down her face. "You mean you are going to take him on?"

Delia walked up to her and grabbed her hand, squeezing in reassurance. "It would be my honor to teach him. You have yourself a very unique and positive little boy in Ozzan and he will make your family proud."

His Mum nodded, breathing heavily as she tried to control the crying. "Yes, he will. I've known all along he would do great things. You have my permission to teach him however you see fit. Let him know I expect him to come home on his free day if only for a bit so he can play with his sisters. They miss him."

"Of course, my dear. Feel free in the evenings to bring the girls around every now and again. Ozzan would love to see them and babies bring happiness wherever they go." She gave his Mum the parchment before making her way out of the garden and back to her shop and the next task of her day.

She smiled as she opened the door to the shop and over-heard Ozzi talking to Shendri, explaining all the different things that humans used that would be foreign to little drag-ons. Carefully, she navigated the shop to avoid the children and snuck into her bedroom. As she crossed the threshold, she took a deep breath turning her mind to what came next.

It had all started five years ago, the bond she had come to rely on and enjoy was suddenly gone. She had fought Immott's decision, especially when she learned that Immott was expecting a baby. She had fantasized about being bonded to a mother dragon and helping to raise the little ones. Yet once she was pregnant, Immott had begun the process of severing ties. It was Delia's fault due to her advancing age, but it was also a problem she couldn't exactly fix. This catastrophic fate delivered so neatly into her lap, however, was reason enough to try her best to get Immott's attention.

She headed straight for her magic work station and began to light the candles that were strategically positioned. She centered her stool in her drawn pentagram on the floor hoping all of the extra measures to amplify her magic would be adequate. She began her deep breathing that was essential to larger, magical workings and fell into her center. She could barely feel Immott's mental state on the outer edges of her magical capability. Using her inner self, she shouted towards where she could hear Immott's consciousness, "I HAVE HER. SHE IS SAFE. MEET AT OUR SPOT."

She repeated these words until they felt seared within her own consciousness. The hours ticked by as she waited, hoping to feel something different from the rage and fear that rippled from Immott's mental energy. Yet nothing changed.

After a few hours of her magical chanting, Delia decided it was time to begin the process of preparing for their trip. She stood slowly, stretched, and went to work gathering magical necessities on the off chance Immott was unwilling to listen.

twelve
Meeting Immott

Wandering into the shop proper, she stopped short looking in awe at the sight before her. In the area of her parlor reserved for patrons waiting on orders or a healing session, sat Shendri. Her body was at full attention. It wasn't something she was used to seeing in a dragon, most of them taking the leadership role within the bonded relationship. Yet, here was Shendri eager to learn from and listen to Ozzi. Delia kept to the shadows of the hall so she could better hear and watch without discovery.

Ozzi stood upon a stool, reaching for a jar on the top shelf. "Aha! There it is." He clambered down the stool and brought the jar close to the lit lamp resting on the window sill. "Rrr-ose. Rose." He turned to look at Shendri as he explained, "That's the first part. Hang on, there's a bit more. Mmm-arr-y. Mary. Rosemary. This is the herb rosemary. She has words written here that explain what it does but they are too small to make out right now." He shrugged and uncorked the jar as he walked toward Shendri. He brought it up to his own nose and wrinkled it a bit before holding it out under Shendri's nose.

Shendri gently bent her head close to the jar to take a large sniff. Ozzi was quick to remove it, which was quite fortuitous since she sneezed abruptly and with such force her tiny body elevated a bit before settling to the floor. Shendri pranced in a circle chirping, though it came out as small puppy yips. Ozzan smiled largely and held the jar out for another sniff. "Perhaps she will teach us all the uses for these things and you can help me find the herbs! You did so good with the mushrooms. Your nose is so sensitive, I'm certain you'll be allowed to help!"

Delia smiled sadly at this last bit. The future was in flux and only time would tell what would be allowed to happen. She cleared her throat causing them both to jump a bit. "Ozzan, I am happy to see you learning your herbs. We must go see about our young charge, though. It's time to meet up with Immott and see what she has to say about this arrangement."

Ozzi paled a bit but nodded and ran to get Shendri's lead. Without comment or prompting, he fastened her up and stood tall while waiting for her to make the first move.

"Alright lad, let's go." She handed him a cloak and helped him fasten it before moving on to secure her own. Then they were off. She led them out of the shop and through the town square until they were out of town. Ozzan remained oddly quiet and Shendri, picking up on the seriousness of the moment, kept the normal prancing antics to a minimum.

Once they passed Ozzi's family home, Delia took them off the normal road and deeper into the forest. Their destination was farther than the cave where she had found the two young ones. They needed to go into the heart of Immott's natural territory. Long ago, when Immott had felt the need to watch over this village, she had claimed the foothills of the mountain range that ringed the valley. Together, Immott and Delia had picked a small rock outcropping as the perfect place to catch up with one another when Delia was still young enough to make the climb regularly.

As they reached the foot of the mountain in question, Delia sketched some runes in the air and a ball of fire appeared floating in front of her. Ozzi gasped and she could feel the questions gathering in his mind but she cut him off. "Another time lad, I shall show you all the secrets but for now we have quite the climb. Go ahead and hand me Shendri's lead. I need you to look around and find me a suitable staff to aid me in my climbing." She could just make out the faint outline of his head as he nodded and did as he was asked. Shendri seemed to be rather apprehensive, glancing around them, with an edginess coming over her. "Here little one, the disguise really isn't needed any longer." She leaned down and sketched the reversal runes and tutted in satisfaction when Shendri once more resembled her normal scaly self.

It didn't take long before Ozzi had returned with a large branch more than adequate to use as a staff. He handed it over with a smile on his face and took back Shendri's lead.

"Alright then, we are heading to that outcropping up there." She pointed up, from this angle they could just make out the bottom half of it. The moon's light causing the bottom to be black in contrast. She looked up and shook her head a bit, it had been years since she had ventured up there. Her shoulders gave a small quiver, imperceptible in the dark as a small voice inside of her claimed they were just ascending the treacherous climb to be eaten but she straightened her shoulders and ordered her inner doubts to quiet.

The ascent took ages, the moon high in the sky by the time they made it. Delia was a bit ashamed as her age showed in the huffing and puffing she was forced to endure. Ozzi, meanwhile, was merely winded. He looked around warily, unsure of what to expect, and Delia remained quiet, waiting to see if Immott had heard her and would decide to show. It wouldn't be a long wait to see her decision.

A voice came from near the mountain face, it was silvery

and dangerous. "What do you think will happen now, Girl? Shall I save your pup just because he has mine?!" Her face slowly came into sight, the light from the moon showing silver on her scales. Her eyes, naturally black, flashed red as she viewed Shendri in the better light of the moon. "She is tied up! HOW DARE YOU!?" Her jaws snapped in anger. The clacking of teeth echoing into the night.

Delia stepped up, placing herself between Ozzi and the silvery head of Immott as the child visibly shook. He dropped the lead and was shaking his head as fear rippled through him. "I..."

Surprisingly, it was Shendri who made the next move. She waddled over, flapping her wings and chittered angrily. Her emotional projections were so loud that even Delia was able to pick them up. Anger, confusion, and sadness all rippled in concert from the little beast as she put herself squarely between Delia and her own mother. Immott's giant head slunk into view low to the ground and hovering above Shendri who batted at it in anger.

Immott snapped her jaws in Shendri's direction but before Delia could comment, Ozzi, fear filling him, screamed, "NO!" He ran around Delia and threw himself on top of the little dragon, the fear of Immott drowned out by his love of his little friend.

Delia raised an eyebrow at Immott and dryly commented, "Hello, old friend, I don't think you need to worry over your pup in our company. The boy will clearly sacrifice himself for a creature far more capable without a second thought. Ozzan, get up, boy! Her mother won't eat her! A bit of discipline is necessary for the young. Do you need your own lesson?"

Ozzi lifted his head and looked at Delia. "Are... are you sure about that? She won't hurt her?" He glanced up at the underside of Immott's jaw and then back to Delia.

Delia wisely swallowed the laugh seeing the seriousness

upon his face. Her own face softened into a smile of understanding, having felt fear for her own bonded partner in the past. "No lad, she won't. I promise."

Slowly, Ozzi stood but he stayed next to Shendri staring at the large head of the dragon before him.

Delia approached Immott's head slowly, unsure of her welcome. "My Great Lady Immott, this is my apprentice Ozzan Madigan, the newly bonded partner to your own daughter. Before you get any ideas, he found her lost and took great care of her. Not once were his intentions of ill nature."

Immott let out a loud dragon huff. "Bonded? They can't be bonded. I've never known a pair to bond as young as they are."

Delia halted her progress toward Immott and nodded slowly. "I, myself, was skeptical but bonded, they are. I am sure Shendri will be happy to explain it to you if you're able to listen."

Immott let out a series of draconic grumbles as she nudged Shendri with her nose. "Out with it, child."

They waited as Shendri began a long series of chirps, whistles, and emotional broadcasts. Ozzi lowered himself to a seated position on the ground, his hand resting on Shendri's back as if encouraging her in her story. Delia smiled at the show of love and support from one so young. It made her yearn for the times when she and Immott were younger and so strongly connected. Quietly, she wiped a tear away and waited for Immott's decision.

Immott turned a beady eye at Delia. "Well old friend, what do we do about this in order to keep their bond? They need to be close, we are proof of that."

As if a light was lit behind Ozzan's eyes, he turned to Delia with a look of awe on his face. "YOU! You were her bonded partner? Wait, but how?"

Delia laughed a bit, covering up her internal mourning of

what once was. She shook her head and opened her mouth to speak but Immott interrupted, "She is still my partner, pup. Questions can follow later. We must find an answer for your predicament now."

Delia nodded to Ozzi before turning her attention to Immott. "Well, we can take turns guarding the pair. I have a few years left in these old bones after all. Plus, I must teach the boy the ways of magic now that he will be gaining his own soon. While they are in town, I shall protect your blood with my own. Then we can all make expeditions together to teach them the ways of the dragon and the unique bonuses of being a bonded pair. It will take some time to convince the men of the village you will no longer eat them."

Immott nodded her head and more of her came into the moonlight as she came closer, the rustle of dark wings sounded above them. "Ah, I fear not the ways of the hunters. Perhaps, though, your plan will be best. Perhaps. Pup!" She turned her attention back to Ozzan. "Will you care for Shendri? Will you protect her from your bloodthirsty counterparts? Human menfolk crave for blood, will you stand against them when it's your time?"

Ozzan sat quietly looking at Shendri before answering. "Miss Immott, if I had to lay down my life to protect hers, I would." His voice shook with deep personal conviction and a lump settled into Delia's throat as emotions clogged her.

Then it dawned on her that they weren't all her own emotions, she was once more connected firmly with Immott. She looked at the dragon, awe on her face before she nodded in understanding. Immott was sacrificing her own mental well-being by reigniting their connection, despite Delia's age, in the hopes that together they could protect this pairing more completely.

Immott spoke in a voice thick, "That'll do, pup. That'll

do. Shendri, my love, will you be okay in the company of the humans? It will be for a few weeks at a time."

Shendri nodded and chirped the feelings of excitement and happiness flooding from her. Ozzan hugged Shendri fiercely around the neck causing a squawk of protest from the little dragon.

Ozzi couldn't believe how lucky he was. His tenth birthday really would go down in history as the best year ever. Shendri had not been taken away from him. Instead Immott had agreed for her to live with him! Most of the time she resembled a puppy rather than a dragon but it was still exciting.

Mistress Delia had worked out a system where in the early morning he would gather the herbs she packaged the night before and take them to the people in need. He gathered the few bags and turned to his new best friend. "Come along, Shendri, this first package is destined for Mr. Wynn."

As he walked through the village everyone gave him a smile. They all seemed less stressed since Immott had finally started letting people come and go from the village. As he arrived at the house Mr. Wynn was seated on his porch watching the comings and goings of the lane. "Ozzi lad. How nice to see you!"

"Hello Mr. Wynn. I brought you some medicines from Mistress Delia." Ozzi lifted the bag helpfully. Shendri pranced in a circle around Ozzi's legs nuzzling and yipping.

"What a lovely little pup you have there. Thank you lad for getting my medicines for me. It's so nice of you." Mr. Wynn took the small bag and placed it on the seat next to him with a small smile.

Ozzi watched his old teacher, concern filling him. "You gonna be okay, Mr. W?"

"I hope so. But ultimately age is catching up with me. All will be well though, Mistress Delia knows her medicines."

Ozzi smiled widely, pride filling him, "She does. Did you know she's going to train me?"

Mr. Wynn matched his smile. "I knew you were destined for great things my lad. Show her just how responsible you are."

Ozzi glowed with praise as he tripped down the stairs waving goodbye as he headed off to the next delivery.

epilogue
A Few Weeks Later

I t was decided between Immott and Delia not to separate the two younglings for fear it would damage their bond and make it harder for Ozzi to participate in his daily life. Immott was also interested to see what the influence of being surrounded by humans would have on her infant daughter.

As an attempt to discourage the hunters from their determined hunting of Immott as retribution for her attacks, she decided to disappear. This disappearance was merely an act, of course, not wanting to be too distant from Shendri or Delia. Instead, she spent her days in the mountains and used the nights to wander about. The hot-headed men of the village made up a story that she had left due to fear of their prowess in hunting. This particular story always gave Delia a coughing fit, her only way to disguise the giggles of incredulity.

Delia utilized her magic to make Shendri's puppy disguise a more permanent situation. She did this by charming an oil that even Ozzan could apply to her before they went out on errands. It had taken some private convincing for Marie to welcome Shendri the Dragon as open armed as she had welcomed Shendri the Puppy but once that task was done, Delia allowed the hatchling to wander about as her true self inside the shop. When customers were about, Shendri got to choose if she was to be a puppy or hidden in Ozzi's room.

Ozzi took to being an apprentice quite nicely. He was eager to learn and, with the added knowledge of his future possibilities, determined to get as much as he could correct. He spent his days, when not learning himself, teaching what he could to Shendri. He was also proving to be quite a talented bonded partner, putting her needs above his own. Surprising everyone, especially Immott, was Shendri's intelligence. She had recently spoken her first words which was years ahead of the draconic learning curve.

Delia, herself, was enjoying the benefits of her reforged bond with Immott. She found the bond to be much stronger than it once had been, resulting in her magic reserves growing. She also wasn't feeling her age as harshly, even managing to keep up with Ozzi most days.

The first expedition for Ozzi to begin learning the ins and outs of dragon care was scheduled for the next day. It worried Delia, him being out in the woods for a full week given his propensity for mischief. She used the excuse that he was off herb gathering, should his parents come calling. Keeping his parents in the dark was one of the hardest parts of this process, especially because of their deep gratitude towards her keeping and caring for Ozzi, allowing them to provide and give more time readily for the twins. In fact, Delia felt that she owed them for the loan of their only son. She had arranged and maintained a small line of credit with all the shops Mistress Madigan frequented in order to aid the family from the shadows.

Her life had gone from rigid and rather sad, the fore-knowledge of her impending death close to her heart, to one of joy and mischief practically overnight. Nightly, she gave thanks to the great beyond for the chance to teach this wonderful pairing and woke each morning excited to see what would become of the day surrounded by the young.

author bio

Mave Hathaway is a writer of fantasy fiction. She contributes to BETA and ARC editing for fellow Indie authors as time allows, eager to aid in supporting fellow authors achieve their dreams of publishing. A prolific writer, she has a series aimed for children; Dragon Legacy, and a series aimed for adults; Baelia. The biggest hope for her writing within the realm that children read, is to give them the confidence to achieve their dreams.

When not writing she is learning how to kick butt in martial arts, and watching movies with her family.

 instagram.com/mavehathaway

acknowledgments

This book and the ones within the Dragon Legacy universe came about when I needed a peaceful escape within my own mind. I started Ozzi's story in 2023 and it has been a whirlwind getting to today. I wouldn't have had the strength to write this if not for the following people.

My husband: In the darkest times of our life together he is the one who encouraged me to write adventures. The specific adventures he has requested are still in production but without his belief I don't think I would have picked up the pen. I am beyond grateful to have had you to ramble bits of this book to.

To my chaos gremlin: You are the perfect office buddy and I hope you enjoy Ozzi. Whenever I got stuck writing I turned to you to ask what he should do next. I hope I do you proud.

My mom: You raised me. You taught me all the ways to survive and without you I simply wouldn't be. I am lucky to have you as my best friend and helper to get this out into the world.

To my sister: You are my biggest cheerleader and have been there for every plot hole and twist. I hope you enjoy this.

To my amazing editors, SplitLeafSaturdays! You were the first people to read this that aren't included in my family. Though you may as well be my book family. I claim you!

Jess always there to save the artistic day! You are awesome!